DRAGONBREATH
NO SUCH THING AS GHOSTS

DRAGONBREATH

NO SUCH THING AS GHOSTS

BY
URSULA VERNON

DIAL BOOKS

an imprint of Penguin Group (USA) Inc.

For Mom. I still think the javelina costume was cool.

DIAL BOOKS
An imprint of Penguin Group (USA) Inc.
Published by The Penguin Group • Penguin Group (USA) Inc., 375 Hudson Street, New York, NY 10014, U.S.A. • Penguin Group (Canada), 90 Eglinton Avenue East, Suite 700, Toronto, Ontario, Canada M4P 2Y3 (a division of Pearson Penguin Canada Inc.) • Penguin Books Ltd, 80 Strand, London WC2R 0RL, England • Penguin Ireland, 25 St. Stephen's Green, Dublin 2, Ireland (a division of Penguin Books Ltd) • Penguin Group (Australia), 250 Camberwell Road, Camberwell, Victoria 3124, Australia (a division of Pearson Australia Group Pty Ltd) Penguin Books India Pvt Ltd, 11 Community Centre, Panchsheel Park, New Delhi - 110 017, India • Penguin Group (NZ), 67 Apollo Drive, Rosedale, Auckland 0632, New Zealand (a division of Pearson New Zealand Ltd) • Penguin Books (South Africa) (Pty) Ltd, 24 Sturdee Avenue, Rosebank, Johannesburg 2196, South Africa • Penguin Books Ltd, Registered Offices: 80 Strand, London WC2R 0RL, England

Designed by Jennifer Kelly
Text set in Stempel Schneidler
Printed in the U.S.A.

10 9 8 7 6 5 4 3 2 1

Library of Congress Cataloging-in-Publication Data
Vernon, Ursula.
No such thing as ghosts / by Ursula Vernon.   p. cm. — (Dragonbreath ; 5)
Summary: Not only must Danny and Wendell trick-or-treat with skeptical classmate Christiana, school bully Big Eddy dares them to enter a haunted house on Halloween night, where they may have to sacrifice their candy to a ghost.
  ISBN 978-0-8037-3527-9 (hardcover)
[1. Halloween—Fiction. 2. Haunted houses—Fiction. 3. Ghosts—Fiction. 4. Bullies—Fiction. 5. Dragons—Fiction. 6. Iguanas—Fiction. 7. Humorous stories.] I. Title.
  PZ7.V5985No 2011
  [Fic]—dc22   2011001164

IN THE DARK OF NIGHT,
THE WILY VAMPIRE STALKS HIS PREY.

THE VAMPIRE MOVES LIKE A SHADOW, LIKE A GHOST. HE MAKES NO SOUND.

THE VAMPIRE CREEPS CLOSER,
PREPARING TO STRIKE AT THE UNSUSPECTING—

PITY CANDY

"Okay," said Danny Dragonbreath, "I give up. What are you supposed to be?"

His best friend, Wendell, sighed. The iguana had a pie plate taped to his chest and was carrying another one.

"I'm a hydrogen atom," said Wendell glumly. He waved the pie plate. "This is my electron."

Danny had only the vaguest idea what an atom or an electron was, but he knew one thing for sure. "You let your mom make your costume, didn't you?"

5

Wendell sighed again.

Danny shook his head. Wendell's mother believed in education the way other parents believed in sports or health food. She also couldn't sew. Danny's mother couldn't sew either, but she understood the importance of Halloween in a young dragon's life and was willing to take him shopping for batwing capes and fake vampire teeth.

"Bummer."

Wendell shrugged.

I'M KIND OF COUNTING ON THE PITY CANDY.

Danny nodded. Pity candy was just as good as any other candy, and there was usually a lot more of it.

"And you're a vampire," said Wendell. "Not bad."

"I wanted to go as a giant false vampire bat, but Mom couldn't find a costume."

Wendell shuddered. There had been an incident with a giant false vampire bat monster over the summer, and while the iguana was more sympathetic to bats in general as a result—was even occasionally glad to see them fly overhead—he wasn't going to get over the giant slavering one any time soon. At least, not until Danny dragged him into something even more horrible, and giant bats started to seem friendly and non-threatening.

That was the nice thing about being friends with Danny—your traumas never had time to settle in.

Danny's father came down the stairs. "Okay, guys, ready to go trick-or-treating? Got your pillowcases?"

"Great! We'll go up and down our street, then drive over to . . ."

He stopped. He gazed at Wendell.

"Wendell, are you a . . . pie salesman?"

"Hydrogen atom," said Wendell wearily.

Danny's father looked briefly at the ceiling and said something under his breath that might have been Wendell's mother's name. "Your mom came up with your costume, didn't she?"

Wendell nodded.

"It's okay," said Wendell. "I'm hoping for the pity candy."

"Oh, well, that's okay then," said Mr. Dragonbreath. He picked up the car keys and called, "Going trick-or-treating, honey!" up the stairs.

"Try not to lose them!" Mrs. Dragonbreath yelled back down.

"Right. Onward! Candy awaits!" He held open the door, and the boys tromped out into the Halloween night.

TRICKING AND TREATING

The Dragonbreaths lived on a quiet street,* and only about half the houses had their lights on, advertising the availability of Halloween candy. One or two had cardboard ghosts on the door or jack-o'-lanterns on the step, but generally Danny's neighbors didn't get into Halloween. The tradition for Danny and Wendell was to trick-or-treat down the block and pick up a few pieces of starter candy. Then Danny's dad would drive them over to the neighborhood in the rich

*Well, quiet except for Danny. The regular parade of ambulances, fire trucks, and emergency plumbers livened up the street substantially, and Danny could never figure out why the neighbors weren't more grateful.

suburb, with the really good candy. Some of the people over there gave out whole candy bars, not the little "fun size" ones. It was not to be missed.

Danny's dad was a good sport about trick-or-treating too, staying well back from Danny and Wendell so that nobody could see that a dad was taking them around. And when he claimed the grown-up candy tax, he usually took things like Milk Duds that no one would want to eat anyway.

The half-dozen houses on Danny's block worked out well for Wendell, because nobody could figure out his costume.

Then they'd drop an extra piece of candy in his bag. Danny, watching the third miniature candy bar land in Wendell's pillowcase, started to regret how good his vampire costume looked.

When they finished the street, they piled into the car, ready for the big haul.

OKAY, GUYS. JUST HAVE TO MAKE ONE STOP . . .

"Where are we stopping?" asked Danny.

"I promised Christiana Vanderpool's mom we'd come over and take her out trick-or-treating," said Mr. Dragonbreath.

"Daaaaaad!"

"What?" Danny's father glanced in the rear-view mirror. "Don't you like Christiana? I thought she brought a sheep brain to school last year."

"Well, yeah," Danny admitted, "that was pretty cool. But . . . she's *weird*."

"I hate to break it to you, but you're kinda weird yourself, son," said his dad.

Wendell snickered.

"Yeah, but . . ." Danny sighed.

What he couldn't say was that Christiana was a Junior Skeptic and didn't even believe he was a dragon. She didn't believe in anything, even stuff like Santa Claus that you weren't really supposed to believe in anymore, but you sort of pretended to because everybody else did. When Ms. Brown had them read "'Twas the Night Before Christmas" in class, Christiana had said it was a Victorian romanticization of an outmoded pagan belief system, and c'mon, that wasn't normal. She sometimes used words even Wendell had to look up.

On the other hand, the sheep brain in the jar *had* been awfully cool.

Danny slouched down in the seat.

"She's probably really nice if you get to know her," his dad said from the front seat.

Which just went to show that grown-ups did not understand a lot of things, because A) Danny had been in school with Christiana for years, and knew her just fine, and B) whatever words you were going to use to describe her, "nice" was not among them.

"Suki liked her," offered Wendell.

"Huh," said Danny. That was unexpected. Suki the salamander had been awesome (even if she was a girl), and if Suki liked Christiana . . . well, anyway, it was only for one night of trick-or-treating. How bad could it be?

THE SKEPTIC

Christiana Vanderpool got into the car wearing a large purple suit and a sarcastic expression. She was a stocky crested lizard shorter than Wendell, although the antenna on her suit made her look taller.

She looked at Danny. "Vampire. Typical." She looked at Wendell. "Mmm. Hydrogen atom?"

Wendell nodded glumly.

"Your electron and your proton aren't in scale," she said, settling herself into the seat.

"I know," said Wendell, who did.

Danny would have said something in defense of his friend—although the pie plates were pretty hard to defend—but his dad got back in the driver's seat, which cut down on the conversation.

"I thought salmon were fish. With . . . like . . . fins and things," said Danny.

"She's the germ that gives you food poisoning," Wendell explained. He looked down his snout at her. "*You're* not to scale either."

Unexpectedly, Christiana grinned. "Yeah, I know. Cool suit though, huh?" She wiggled her cilia at them.

It was a short drive to the really good neighborhood, and bands of kids were already roaming the streets. Danny scrambled out of the car, followed by the others. The nearest house had a strobe light and a smoking cauldron. The sound of recorded hysterical laughter echoed down the sidewalk. It was perfect.

ALL RIGHT, ALL RIGHT. YOU GUYS KNOW THE DRILL. I'LL STAND BACK HERE AND LOOK UNCOOL.

DAAAAAAD...

The trio settled into a pattern. Christiana rang the doorbell. The door opened, and Danny pushed Wendell forward. Wendell held out his pillowcase and looked hopeful, whereupon the homeowner gazed at the iguana's pie plates, was seized by pity, and dumped candy with a generous hand.

By the time they'd walked up one side of the street and two cul-de-sacs, Wendell's pillowcase was dragging on the ground. Christiana and Danny weren't quite so fortunate, but they still had very respectable hauls. Danny was beginning to wish he'd brought a second pillowcase.

They'd also encountered boiling cauldrons, shrieking hinges, animatronic skeletons, over-stuffed scarecrows, and three more strobe lights. The flashing lights caused Wendell to mutter darkly about seizures and made Danny's father do a horribly embarrassing dance that he said was called "The Robot."

Still, it had been a good night. At least until—

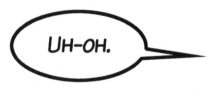

Danny and Christiana followed Wendell's gaze and made identical "ungh" noises.

Big Eddy the Komodo dragon and his cronies were walking up the sidewalk toward them.

"Hold on to your candy," muttered Christiana.

Danny looked over his shoulder, to where his dad was talking to some other parents, probably about doing The Robot. The presence of nearby adults would keep Big Eddy from beating them up and taking their candy . . . probably . . . but it was dark enough out that you didn't want to take any chances.

"C'mon," said Wendell, pointing at another knot of kids coming up the sidewalk behind them. "Safety in numbers."

Danny was willing to give it a try. They slowed their footsteps up to the next house, and pretended to be very interested in a couple of jack-o'-lanterns lining the next porch. By the time they reached the street again, the other kids were only a few feet behind them.

"Oh look," said Big Eddy, "it's dorkbreath and his sidekick." He loomed over Danny, who backed up, not wanting to get shoved. "Got tired of pretending to be a dragon and decided to be a vampire, huh?"

"I *am* a dragon," said Danny, but he said it under his breath. He had a fond memory of a rat riding Big Eddy down a hallway, and preferred not to tarnish it with a memory of Big Eddy's fist hitting him in the snout.

Christiana gave him a skeptical look. Danny felt his scales get hot.

"Nothing," said Wendell wretchedly as Big Eddy yanked away his electron pie plate.

The other kids had arrived. Danny recognized a few of them from school, although they were mostly in other grades. None of them seemed to want to press past Big Eddy, but the sidewalk was getting awfully crowded.

Somebody pushed Danny in the back, not hard, but enough to move him forward a little. Big Eddy's eyes snapped back to Danny. Danny winced.

"I'm surprised you weren't too scared to come out, dorkbreath. Aren't you afraid a ghost's gonna get you?"

"I'm not scared of any stupid ghosts," said Danny, stepping off the curb and circling around Big Eddy. Maybe if they started walking away, the bully would forget about them. Big Eddy didn't have a very long attention span.

No such luck. The big Komodo dragon turned around and started following him. The other kids followed at a cautious distance.

"You're totally scared," said Big Eddy. "You're a big chicken."

"So prove it," said Big Eddy. "I bet you're too scared to go up to the haunted house."

Danny rolled his eyes. "I've *been* to haunted houses. They're not scary.* It's just people in masks."

"Not *that* kind of haunted house, dorkbreath. A real one. That one." Big Eddy spun around and pointed.

"How do you know the house is haunted?" asked Christiana. "It just looks abandoned to me."

"*Everybody* knows it's haunted," said Big Eddy.

"Then *everybody* ought to have proof," said Christiana.

Big Eddy looked confused, which was generally a prelude to Big Eddy getting mad. Danny jumped in. "Anyway, even if it is haunted, we can't go in. It's trespassing."

The Komodo dragon sneered at him. "You're just chicken."

---

*Actually, this was not entirely true. There was a place way out in the country that put on a haunted house and hayride that had guys in ski masks carrying chain saws, and even though you *knew* they were actors, the sound of the chain saw starting up in the dark was pretty terrifying. Danny had made his parents go through it three times.

31

"I'm not chicken," said Danny, "but my dad is back there"—he jerked a thumb in the direction of his father and the other grown-ups—"and I can't just break into somebody's house in front of him. He'd ground me for a *month*."

There was a murmur of agreement from the kids gathered around them. You couldn't do that sort of thing in front of grown-ups. They really didn't understand.

"So go trick-or-treat it," said Big Eddy, shoving Danny in the shoulder. "Prove you're not chicken."

Danny gulped.

It occurred to him that having all the other kids around might mean that there were more witnesses if Big Eddy decided to beat him up . . . but it also meant that there were more witnesses to Big Eddy calling him a chicken.

He looked up at the house. The driveway was long and dark and overhung with trees. There were no lights on and the windows were boarded up.

He looked back toward his dad, but apparently the grown-ups were having a really interesting conversation about life insurance or vegetables or something else of interest to grown-ups. They were definitely not paying attention except for an occasional glance to make sure the kids weren't being hit by cars.

"Bet you won't," said Big Eddy. "Bet you're scared."

"I am NOT," said Danny, which was mostly true. He wasn't scared of ghosts, exactly—they couldn't be that much worse than a giant squid—but he wasn't sure how you dealt with them. Ghosts could go all invisible and stuff, and they probably weren't bothered by having fire breathed on them.

I'D TOTALLY DO IT!

SO DO IT!

It occurred to Danny that he had possibly backed himself into a bit of a corner.

"Um . . ."

"I'll come with you," said Christiana firmly. "I don't believe in ghosts."

The crowd of kids all took a step back. Saying you didn't believe in ghosts on Halloween was kind of like standing in a thunderstorm and saying you didn't believe in lightning.

Danny was stuck. If Christiana was going, and Big Eddy was watching . . . well, there was nothing else to do. He slung his pillowcase of candy over his shoulder, cast a last longing look back at his dad—no help there—and started walking.

Wendell found himself with a dilemma.

He could go with Danny and Christiana, who were probably about to be mauled by ghosts, or he could stay here. With Big Eddy.

You might believe in ghosts or not—but the school bully was definitely real. And Wendell had stuck by Danny in worse situations than just haunted houses . . . there had been the squid, and the sewers, and the giant bat, and the thing with the ninjas . . .

The iguana sighed and scurried after Danny and Christiana, up the long driveway to the (possibly) haunted house.

PANIC TIME

The house looked even worse close up. The porch was sagging, the windows were boarded, and there were real cobwebs, even thicker and denser than the fake Halloween kind. Danny's parents had always said that you weren't supposed to go to a house that didn't have the lights on, and this place didn't even have bulbs in the porch light.

"It sure looks haunted," said Danny.

Wendell gulped.

"Nobody's ever proved that ghosts exist," said Christiana, striding determinedly toward the door.

"I have a hard time breathing fire under pressure," said Danny. (Actually, under pressure seemed to be the only time he *could* breathe fire—if by "pressure" you meant "stark raving terror"—but this was a difficult distinction to explain to somebody like Christiana.)

She smirked. "Yeah, that's what they all say."

"*I've* seen him breathe fire," said Wendell staunchly.

YOU'RE HIS BEST FRIEND. YOU'RE NOT A RELIABLE WITNESS.

Any gratitude Danny might have been feeling to Christiana for coming with them was evaporating rapidly. He gritted his teeth and stomped up the steps onto the porch.

"No doorbell," said Wendell. "Nobody's here. Can we go back now?"

"I guess we could knock," said Danny. "I mean . . . nobody's gonna come, but as long as we knock, that ought to be enough . . ."

He made a fist and rapped on the peeling paint of the door. The sound seemed to boom through the inside of the house, much more loudly than it should have. Wendell cringed.

"Well," said Christiana, "I guess that—"

With a long wooden moan, the door swung open.

Danny knew he should turn around right now and walk away, at least until he was off the porch, and then he should run like his tail was on fire.

It was Halloween that made him do it, he decided later. On any other day of the year, he would have run away, but on Halloween, you went up to scary haunted houses and the doors creaked open and that was *normal*.

He took a step forward, onto the threshold.

"Danny, what are you doing?" squeaked Wendell.

Christiana, however, stepped up beside him and poked her head around the edge of the door frame.

"Must've been unlocked," she said. "What a dump!"

As if in a dream, Danny took another step forward, into the dark room. There was moonlight coming around the edges of the boarded windows, casting long, pale stripes across the floor.

DANNY—

WHOOOOOMPH!

The door slammed shut. It knocked Wendell into Christiana, and both of them into the room, pinching Wendell's tail cruelly in the door frame. He yelped. Danny jumped.

"What happened?" yelled Wendell, scrambling to his feet. "Why'd it close!?"

"It was just the wind," said Christiana, grabbing for the doorknob. "Don't freak out."

She turned the doorknob and pushed.

Nothing happened.

She shoved at it harder, twisting the knob back and forth, but the door didn't budge.

"Um," she said.

Danny pushed her aside and grabbed the doorknob himself.

"It's stuck!" he said.

"We're going to die . . ." Wendell moaned. "We're trapped . . ."

Danny slammed his shoulder against the door, which did more damage to his shoulder than the door. It didn't budge.

"We're not stuck," said Danny. "We just need to find another way out." He peered around the room.

There was a dark fireplace and a sofa covered by an old sheet, neither of which was any help at all. Most of the windows were still intact, but at least one was broken out, leaving a frame edged with daggers of glass that glittered in the moonlight. If they tried to go out through the window, they'd have to find a way to break the boards out, then crawl through without disemboweling themselves on the broken glass.

This did not seem promising.

"There's got to be a back door," said Christiana.

A dark doorway led deeper into the house. While moonlight lit their room unevenly, the hallway beyond the door was pitch-black.

"I'm not going in there!" said Wendell.

Danny couldn't blame him. The doorway looked like an open mouth. He rubbed the back of his neck nervously. "Do the lights work?"

Christiana found a light switch and flicked it a few times. Nothing happened.

FLIP
FLIP
FLIP

"I was afraid of that," said Danny. "Um. I don't have a flashlight . . ."

"Me neither."

Wendell coughed. "Err . . . wait. Mom made me bring one. . . ." He dug around in his pillowcase of candy and eventually pulled out a flashlight. "She was worried that if it got dark I'd get hit by a car."

"I take back everything I've ever said about your mother," said Danny, grabbing the flashlight.

WAIT— WHAT HAVE YOU SAID ABOUT MY MOTHER?

The flashlight didn't work. Danny unscrewed the cap to check the batteries. Behind him, he heard Christiana say, "Periodic table bandages, huh?"

"Yeah."

"My dad gets the countries-of-the-world ones. I got a splinter in my hand last month and spent three days staring at the gross national product of Belgium."

Wendell laughed. It was a nervous, strangled sort of laugh, but it was still a laugh. Danny, whose knowledge of Belgium began and ended with waffles, poured the batteries into his hand, blew on them, and shoved them back in the flashlight. He smacked the flashlight into his palm a few times, and it lit up grudgingly.

The little circle of light seemed very small against the darkness. Danny flicked the light down the hallway, over the dusty floorboards, revealing another open doorway.

"I guess we have to go down there," he said.

He took a step forward.

THE HAUNTED BATHROOM

A shriek echoed through the house, a horrible keening noise that sank to a dull moan and finally died away. It sounded like somebody being tortured. A shriek from Wendell followed, although it wasn't quite as loud. Danny jumped.

"What was *that*?!" he said.

"It's the ghost," said Wendell, arms over his head. "It knows we're coming, it's gonna get us, we're gonna dieeeee. . . ."

"Ha!" said Christiana suddenly. She strode forward into the hallway and stomped on the floor.

Another shriek rang out, shorter this time.

"It's not a ghost, it's the floor," she said. She bounced up and down on a particularly creaky board, producing a series of short groaning noises, like a donkey with hiccups. "I bet nobody's walked on it in *years*."

Danny rolled his eyes, feeling embarrassed. He hadn't been scared. Not exactly. Startled, maybe. It had been loud, that was all. He stepped onto the floorboard, which yelped again.

"What if the ghost heard it?" asked Wendell.

"There are no ghosts," said Christiana. "Nobody's ever proved ghosts exist, anyway."

DO THE GHOSTS KNOW THAT?

Wendell was generally pretty scientifically minded, but he'd seen too many weird things while hanging around with Danny. Also, he'd checked out a book of ghost stories from the library a week ago, and it had some pretty alarming stuff in it. There had been one about a hitchhiker who turned out to be a ghost who always came back on the anniversary of her death. It made his scales crawl.

Danny took another few steps down the hallway and reached an open doorway on the left wall. He shone the light into it. Christiana and Wendell came up behind him, the iguana taking big steps to avoid the creaky floorboard. The room was a bathroom, and it was *nasty*.

Ewwwwww . . .

The toilet was missing a lid, and the water was rust-brown and slimy. The paint was peeling and had formed big blisters, and some of the blisters had burst. Mold crept up the walls.

There was a picture of a clown over the toilet tank. The clown was crying, which was probably meant to be tragic, but was mostly just creepy.

"If there's a ghost here, they're a real slob," said Danny.

"How long did you leave that sandwich in your locker that one time?" asked Wendell. "Purely as a matter of curiosity . . ."

"Yeah, but it was a sandwich. Not a whole *bathroom*." (The sandwich in question had turned a variety of interesting colors and then grown fur. He'd thrown it away eventually, although Wendell claimed that it was alive and trying to communicate.)

I GUESS THAT'S FAIR . . .

They retreated from the bathroom. Wendell said under his breath, "I hear clown attacks are up this year . . ."

"I'm pretty sure I can kick your tail, Wendell," said Christiana through gritted teeth. Danny snickered.

The young crested lizard shut the bathroom door behind them. When the boys looked at her, she said, "What?"

"Afraid the clown will sneak up on us?" asked Danny.

"Look," said Christiana, sounding annoyed, "I just don't—"

The bathroom door swung slowly open. The three of them stared at it. "Maybe it didn't latch," said Danny, because somebody had to say something.

"The door frame's probably warped," said Christiana nervously. She wiped her hands on the sides of her bacteria suit.

"Yeah," said Danny. "Still . . ." He took a deep breath and shone the flashlight back into the bathroom.

Nothing. The paint was still peeling, the toilet was still disgusting, the painting of flowers over the toilet was still—

"Didn't that used to be a clown?" asked Danny.

Christiana actually took the flashlight away from him and shone it on the painting, which was of a vase full of flowers.

"Well," she said, after a minute, and then stopped. She looked up and down the hall, as if expecting there to be another bathroom, possibly with a clown painting in it.

"I don't know." She frowned. "I suppose we might not have seen it clearly the first time, but I sure *thought* it was a clown . . ."

Danny didn't know what to think. It had definitely been a clown, and it was definitely *not* a clown now. At the same time, it seemed like a weird thing for a ghost to do. Ghosts were supposed to rattle chains and moan, not switch around the artwork.

"Anyway," said Christiana, sounding a little more confident, "just because we can't explain it doesn't mean there isn't an explanation. It just means that we don't know what it is right now."

"Uh-huh," said Wendell. "This sounds like a great philosophical discussion. Maybe we could have it sometime. You know, maybe when we're not *standing in the hallway of a haunted house*?!"

Christiana looked at Danny. Danny looked at Christiana.

"Right!" said Danny. "Back door. Let's find it."

SOMETHING'S HUNGRY

The kitchen lay at the end of the hallway. Danny felt for a light switch and flicked it hopefully, even though he was pretty sure it wouldn't work.

It didn't. Wendell sighed.

In the beam of the flashlight, they saw stairs leading up to the second story. All three of them moved away from the stairs. The rest of the kitchen looked ordinary, if dusty—stove, sink, refrigerator, all dark and dim and silent. The linoleum was peeling up in the corners and the window over the sink was boarded up.

"We don't know that anybody died here," said Christiana. "They might have just moved out."

"They could have moved out because it was haunted!" Wendell waved his pie plate in the air. "I read a book about this one haunted house where they had poltergeists and they tried everything to get them out and the poltergeists kept making weird noises and turning on the faucets and the people had to move."

Danny had an urge to borrow this book from Wendell, which did not happen often. Christiana was less impressed.

"You're being irrational," she said, folding her arms. "None of that stuff is real."

Wendell opened his mouth to say that after several years of running around with Danny, he'd seen giant squid and ninja frogs, were-hot-dogs and ancient bat gods, and his notion of what was possible had expanded quite a bit as a result. But then he closed it again, without saying anything. Christiana would demand that he prove it, and he couldn't prove anything standing in a dark kitchen in an abandoned and probably haunted house.

He wished he could. A few years ago, he would have agreed with her. Now she just thought he was stupid, and Wendell really hated it when people thought he was stupid.

"I think there's a door through here," said Danny, pointing the flashlight through another doorway.

They walked as quietly as they could, practically sneaking. Even Christiana was doing it. There was something about the empty house that made you not want to make loud noises.

On the far wall of the new room was a closed door with a window in it. The window was boarded over, but it looked like it might lead to the outside.

Wendell rushed forward and grabbed the handle. All three kids held their breath.

The handle turned. The deadbolt did not. Wendell threw himself back, clinging to the handle, and only succeeded in making the door rattle in its frame.

Danny said a word that his mother said occasionally when somebody cut her off in traffic.

Wendell slumped against the door frame. "Do you think your dad will find us? It's been *hours*."

"It's been about twenty minutes," said Christiana. "And he'd have to figure out what house we went to. Unless Big Eddy tells him, he won't know."

BIG EDDY?
WE'RE DOOMED.

"Maybe we could break a window," said Danny. "Like . . . with a chair or something." He hated the thought of breaking a window—mostly because he *knew* it was going to come out of his allowance—but if there wasn't any other way out . . .

"It occurs to me—" began Christiana.

Wendell said, ". . . Eep."

Danny followed the iguana's gaze and felt his stomach do an unpleasant sort of flop.

An enormous white shape was looming up behind Christiana, nearly twice as tall as she was. Pale lumps, like arms or wings, flared out to either side.

"Oh," said Wendell, "oh, oh—"

"Christiana," hissed Danny, "behind you!" He lifted the flashlight with nerveless fingers. The vast shape seemed to rise even higher.

Christiana spun around, blinked, and then made an exasperated noise.

"Come *on,* you guys . . ."

She reached out, caught a corner of the shape, and yanked.

The sheet came off the ancient wingback chair in a cloud of dust.

"It's a *chair*," she said. "It's not scary."

"I find that upholstery rather alarming," said Wendell, eyeing the garish floral pattern.

"I can't believe you guys. Every little noise and it's 'Oh, help, it's a ghost, it's a poltergeist!'"

"It's dark," said Danny indignantly, "and the white sheet, it really *did* look like a ghost."

"I keep telling you, there's no such thing as—"

She was cut off by the sound of footsteps. Loud, heavy footsteps, coming from upstairs. All three kids froze, listening as someone—or something—walked overhead.

A door opened and shut. Then silence . . .

. . . or not quite silence.

"*Hungry . . .*" whispered a soft, hissing voice. It didn't sound very close, but it wasn't exactly far away, either. "*I'm hungry . . .*"

"I don't know if that was a ghost," whispered Danny, "but there's definitely somebody up there."

THUDS AND FOOTSTEPS

Danny looked at Wendell. Wendell looked at Danny. Christiana looked at both of them.

Wendell opened his mouth to say something— probably "We're all going to die," or something equally upbeat—but never got the words out.

Something began hammering violently on the back door. It sounded like thunder, like drums, like a herd of horses running up the side of the building.

Most of all, it sounded like something wanted in. Bad.

Wendell shrieked, dropped his candy, and bolted. Danny took off after him—to make sure he didn't trip in the dark. Yeah. Absolutely. Not because he was terrified. Definitely not.

They skidded into the front room. Danny thought for a second that Wendell might run right *through* the front door, leaving a cut-out opening behind him, like a cartoon. They hoped the footsteps behind them were Christiana's. (If they weren't Christiana's, Danny didn't want to know.)

Another flurry of pounding shook the house, this time on the *front* door. Wendell let out another ear-splitting shriek and stopped so fast that Danny ran into his back. More hammering hit the boarded windows, making the glass rattle in the frames.

"We're surrounded," moaned Wendell, backing toward the hallway. "There's no way out . . ."

Danny didn't know what was going on, but he was pretty sure he didn't like it.

He inhaled, feeling smoke roil at the bottom of his lungs. He didn't know if there was anything there to breathe fire on, or whether he'd just burn the house down, but he was going to be prepared.

"It's the ghost!" said Wendell.

"Maybe it's vampires!" said Danny.

"Maybe it's your dad trying to find us," said Christiana.

Hammer-blows struck both the front and back doors. It sounded like the doors would fall down at any second.

"Hungry . . ." hissed the spectral voice, practically in their ears.

It was kind of ironic, Danny thought—just a minute ago, he'd wanted the doors to open, and now he wanted them to stay closed.

"Here!" whispered Christiana beside him. "Get the other end!" She grabbed one side of the couch and tried to drag it toward the door.

Danny tossed the flashlight to Wendell, who promptly dropped it. (Wendell always did catch like a nerd.) The light spun crazily over the ceiling as Danny threw himself at the other end of the couch.

Between the two of them, they managed to drag the couch so that the end was in front of the door.

"I don't know how long that'll hold," Danny panted, watching the couch vibrate with every blow.

"We've got to hide," gasped Wendell, clutching his pie plate to his chest.

"We should—um—retreat and gather more data," said Christiana.

They fled down the hallway.

NOT UPSTAIRS! THEY'RE UPSTAIRS!

Danny didn't know who "they" were, and didn't feel like finding out. He grabbed for the door to his right and yanked it open.

Stairs led down into the dark. Danny hesitated and shot another look at the front door.

The pounding started up again, from both the front and back. Christiana spread her hands and shook her head, clearly out of ideas.

"*Do* something . . ." moaned Wendell.

Gulping, Danny pulled Wendell down onto the first step and waited for Christiana to follow. He reached past the crested lizard and closed the door behind them.

It closed with a sinister *thunk!* shutting the three of them inside the cellar.

RAT LEADER

The sounds were much more muffled inside the cellar. Danny turned and shined the flashlight down the stairs.

The floor was concrete, not very clean. Cobwebs hung thickly from the ceiling. An old washer and dryer stood in one corner, surrounded by rusty water stains. The other side of the basement was full of old boxes.

"Guess we should go down," Danny whispered.

They went down, wedged so closely together that it was a wonder they didn't trip each other,

fall down the stairs, break their necks and save the ghosts the trouble.

If it *was* ghosts.

"I don't think it was ghosts," said Christiana.

Wendell jumped at her voice, and Danny had to grab for the banister.

"If it wasn't ghosts, then why did you run?" he snapped.

"Because it was freaky!" she shot back. "I happen to believe in serial killers and cannibals, thank you very much!"

"Don't forget clowns," muttered Wendell.

Christiana gave him a look that would have burned through his pie plate, if he hadn't dropped it in the headlong flight to the cellar. He prudently decided to stand on the other side of Danny.

"You think it was cannibals?" asked Danny. "Cool! I always wanted to meet a real cannibal..." He ran the flashlight over the boxes. Most of them had things written on the side like "Summer clothes" and "Kitchen stuff," but then again,

if you were a cannibal, you probably didn't put labels like "Yummy dead bodies" and "Fresh corpses" on your boxes, did you?

After all, if you used a moving company, they were bound to get suspicious—

"No, I don't think it was cannibals," said Christiana. "Let's look at this logically."

She paced back and forth at the foot of the stairs. Danny backed up a step.

"Who knows we're in this house?" she asked.

"The trick-or-treaters behind us," said Danny.

"Big Eddy," said Wendell.

"Bingo." She pointed at Wendell. "And who would think it was hysterical if we were locked up in this house?"

"He probably snuck back here to scare us," she said.

Danny nodded. "And then he and his buddies—you know, the two losers he hangs around with—started pounding on the doors."

Wendell frowned. "Then how do you explain the footsteps upstairs? Or that voice?"

"One of them could have snuck in," said Christiana. "Or even waited for us upstairs. He might even be the one who locked us in. And maybe he just hasn't had dinner yet."

"It makes sense," said Danny. He felt like an idiot. And he was slightly disappointed he wouldn't get to meet a cannibal.

HE'S THE ONE WHO DARED US TO COME UP HERE.

"No," said Wendell, after a minute, "the *point* is that if someone got in up there, there must be a way out too, right?"

Christiana frowned. "Not necessarily. Isn't one of his buddies a chameleon? He could have hidden downstairs . . ."

"He could have, but I bet there's an open window or something upstairs." Wendell thought about it. "You'd think Big Eddy would have gotten in too, though . . ."

"He's the size of a moose," said Christiana disdainfully.

Danny slapped his forehead. "You're right! He might not have been able to fit in a window—but I bet we could!"

Christiana nodded. "It's worth checkin—EEEP!"

She jumped about six inches sideways and into a box marked "Kitchen." Danny spun around, prepared to see anything from Big Eddy to a cannibalistic clown from Mars, and saw—

IT'S ONLY A RAT.

"You brought a sheep brain to school, but you're scared of *rats*?" asked Wendell.

"I'm not scared of rats," muttered Christiana, extracting herself from the pile of boxes she'd fallen into. A large copper bowl rolled in a circle, teetering, and stopped with a faint *booonnng*.

"Rats are highly intelligent and serve a valuable place in the ecosystem. I was just startled," she said. "I was looking over there, and it moved, and . . . look, it's been a rough night, okay?"

Danny put his hands on his knees and addressed the rat. "Hey there! Do you know our friend the potato salad?"

The rat hopped into the cardboard boxes and vanished for a moment. It returned, looked Danny up and down, and shook its whiskers. "Squeak."

"Nothing we can fit through," Danny guessed. "Crud."

"You're talking to a rat," said Christiana.

"Hey, you *said* they were highly intelligent," said Danny. "We've had good luck with rats."

Christiana rubbed her forehead, looked like she was about to say something scathing about rats, changed her mind, and said instead, "If we're staying down here, I'm taking off my head."

This was the sort of statement that would normally have required a great deal of analysis and caused concern, but then she reached up and pulled the head off her costume. "Phew. That thing is *hot*."

"Squeak?"

Danny looked over. The rat had returned, and was perching on the edge of a box, at eye level.

"Hey again," he said to the rat.

"Squeak!" it said. It made a beckoning gesture, then ran down the box to the floor.

HERE WE GO AGAIN . . .

HEY, FOLLOWING THE RAT WORKED LAST TIME!

SQU-EAK!

The rat hopped from box to box, and finally darted through a hole in the back wall. Danny played the flashlight over the hole and saw the frame of a low, square door.

"It's a hidden passage!" he said. "Cool!" Danny approved of hidden passages. You could hide treasure in them, or smugglers or skeletons. Or maybe even all three.

"It's just a crawlspace," said Christiana. "Probably so people can work on the plumbing."

"I am *not* going in there," said Wendell.

The rat poked its head out again and squeaked.

"Let's see if we can get it open," said Danny. He knelt and tugged on the door. It stuck a bit, then yawned open.

The crawlspace was dark and cobwebby and smelled like rotted wood and his aunt Shirley's casserole. The rat ran a few feet down and squeaked again.

"Maybe it's a way out," said Danny. He stuck his head through the doorway. The rat squeaked excitedly. Wood creaked under Danny's hands.

Wendell fidgeted. On the one hand, Danny was going into the hideous unknown darkness. On the other hand, he was taking the flashlight with him. "Danny . . ."

"I'm fine," Danny called. "Stinks in here, though. Smells all moldy."

"Some mold spores can be really toxic," Christiana said helpfully.

"Neat!" Danny said over his shoulder. "Can we throw them at the ghost?"

Wendell wrung his hands.

"Are you okay!?" Wendell rushed forward. He could just make out Danny lying on a pile of boxes down below.

"I'm . . . fine . . . I think . . ." Danny sat up, rubbing his head groggily. "Guess the junk broke my fall . . ."

The rat, squeaking worriedly, flipped over the broken edges of the boards and dropped into the opening below. A minute later, the rat and Danny were eye to eye.

Christiana shouldered Wendell aside and peered over the edge of the hole. "Looks like you're in some kind of sub-basement," she said. "Must have been another storage room. I don't think we can pull you up, but maybe we can find the stairs and meet you down there."

"Okay." Danny sat up. The pile of boxes made some interesting sproinging and twanging noises. "Man, they sure had a lot of junk . . ." He found the flashlight and swept it around the room. "Gotta be a door somewhere . . ."

The rat caught his attention again. It was waving him over to one side of the room.

"Is that the door?"

Moving through the pile of debris was harder than Danny expected. He couldn't walk. Instead he made a series of lunges, crushing boxes and old magazines underfoot. It was like swimming in a sea of moldy cardboard.

When Danny finally reached the rat, it was perched on the lip of a box next to the wall. It squeaked at him, and pointed.

"What's down there?" Danny trained the light down, through a gap in the boxes, and saw . . . something. It looked faded and fuzzy and rather grungy.

The rat squeaked again, very seriously, and pointed up at the ceiling, then back down at the object.

Danny had no idea what that meant, but if the rat thought it was important . . . He dropped to his knees and reached for whatever it was.

It was a stuffed animal.

It was impossible to tell what it had been—a bear, maybe, or a sheep, or something else. It had a generic animal shape, and one dusty button eye.

The rat squeaked again.

"This?" Danny turned it over, puzzled. "What's so important about—"

And then the world went away.

DANNY GETS FLOATY

Danny was floating in a dark place.

This did not bother him as much as it could have. He didn't seem to have a body, but hey, these things happened. Maybe he was dreaming, or he'd hit his head harder than he thought and now he was having an out-of-body experience. He'd seen a TV show about those. There had been weird floaty music on the show, and he was a bit disappointed that there wasn't any music now.

Still, you couldn't have everything.

A door opened, and light spilled into the room. At first Danny thought Wendell and Christiana had found him, but he seemed to be looking down on the door, and the light coming through the doorway was shining on a bedroom, not a pile of junk.

"How are you feeling, honey?" asked an unfamiliar voice.

Danny wasn't sure if she was talking to him, and furthermore wasn't sure how to talk in his bodiless state, but fortunately somebody else answered, so it didn't matter.

"I'm *fine,* Mom," said a little kid's voice. It sounded crabby and tired and sort of thick. Then it started coughing.

"Oh, honey . . ." said the mom, and she walked from the doorway, across Danny's vision to the bed. "I'm making you breakfast. It's eggs."

There was a kid in the bed, Danny could see. It was only about the size of Danny's seven-year-old cousin. Danny couldn't tell if it was a boy

or a girl, but he could definitely tell that it was grumpy.

"Don't want eggs. I wanna go trick-or-treating," it said, folding its arms.

"Honey, you're too sick to go out," said the mom. "I know it's disappointing . . ."

"I wanna GO!"

Come to think of it, it kinda *sounded* like his seven-year-old cousin too.

"Honey—"

"I WANNA!"

Fortunately a full-blown tantrum was broken off by a coughing fit. It was a bad cough too, the kind that had bubbly snotty stuff in it.

Danny tried to see if he could move around without a body. He thought he managed to wobble back and forth a bit, but it was hard to tell.

He wondered what the people below him would see if they looked up—a ghostly dragon hanging around the ceiling? Nothing at all?

"I *like* trick-or-treating," said the little kid. "I hate eggs. You're *mean*."

"I know it seems mean," said the mom, "but you're sick. Next year you can go out. Won't that be fun?"

She bustled around the bed, tucking something in alongside the kid. Danny caught the gleam of familiar button eyes.

"Don't wanna go next year . . ." said the little kid, hugging the stuffed animal. "Wanna go *now* . . ."

The scene was fading. Danny had a sense that there was something important here, something he was supposed to remember, and he tried to grab for it, but it was like having a dream and waking up and trying to remember—

—and then he was back in the basement, staring into the dusty eye of the stuffed animal.

"Whoa!" he said. He patted himself down—yup, that was his body, all right, and he seemed to be back in it. "That was *awesome!* Did I just have an out-of-body experience?"

The rat spread its paws and shrugged.

"I gotta tell Wendell!"

OPERATION MONGOOSE!

Wendell would have liked nothing better than to be having a long talk about out-of-body experiences with Danny. Instead, he was trying to find his way to the basement stairs in the pitch-black.

The next ten minutes were not among the best of Wendell's life.

He and Christiana ran into each other. They ran into the boxes. Christiana yelled at him. He yelled back. They flung junk aside and hit each other with it. Christiana upended an entire box of plastic forks on Wendell's head. (She claimed it was an accident. The iguana had his suspicions.)

Finally, they saw a rectangle of light.

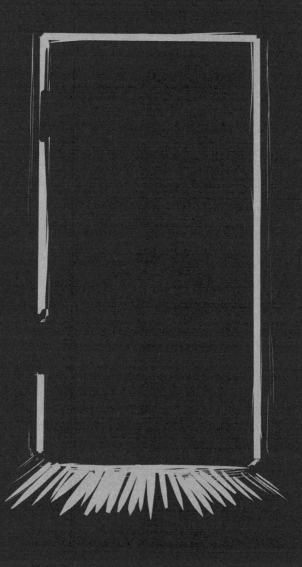

And once they got close to the door, they could hear Danny on the other side.

Eventually, with Danny pushing from his side and Wendell and Christiana pulling on their side, they got the door open.

"I missed you! I missed you so much!" Wendell cried.

"Uh—" said Danny.

Wendell snatched the flashlight away from him and hugged it. "Never leave me again," he told the light.

". . . right, then," said Danny. "Guys, you're not gonna believe this. I found this stuffed animal, and I had this vision—and I think I know what we're up against."

"You're right, I don't believe it," said Christiana.

"I'm not saying you didn't see something," said the iguana. "It could have been a vision. But you did fall and hit your head, and there *were* all those mold spores . . ."

Danny sighed. He should have known that

Christiana wouldn't believe anything like a vision, but he had to admit that Wendell's defection stung a little. Danny glared at the stuffed whatever-it-was. "The rat thought it was important," he said stubbornly.

"Look," said Christiana, "this should be easy. We'll do what scientists do. We'll get proof."

HOW DO YOU PROVE A VISION?

"We can't prove something like that," said Christiana, "but it should be easy to prove whether it's Big Eddy making the noise and not a ghost." She started up the stairs, and Danny and Wendell followed her into the hallway.

They didn't dare use the flashlight, for fear of giving themselves away. Danny stepped carefully over the creaky board, and Christiana and Wendell stopped next to it.

Danny knelt down by one of the windows and listened carefully.

After a minute or two, he heard somebody say, "I'm bored." It sounded like Jason the salamander, one of Big Eddy's cronies.

"Shut up," hissed a deeper voice. Danny jerked back from the window, startled—from the sound

of it, Big Eddy was standing directly on the other side of the wall.

"They're probably freaking out in there," said Big Eddy. "When they're good and scared, we'll throw open the door and they'll go running. Then we can grab their candy and get out of here."

"Couldn't you just have taken their candy?" asked Jason.

SHUT UP.
I DON'T JUST
WANT THE CANDY,
I WANNA MAKE
DORKBREATH
PEE HIS
PANTS.

Danny rolled his eyes.

"They haven't made a noise for *ages,*" said Jason. "Maybe they left."

"Shut up, or I'll take *your* candy."

Danny sighed. It looked like Christiana was right—but then what was the meaning of his vision in the basement? Why had the rat led him there? It didn't make *sense.*

He looked over his shoulder. Christiana and Wendell were waiting in the hallway. Clearly they'd both heard Big Eddy talking too. He tiptoed back to join them,.

"So," said Wendell. "What do we do now? Wait until Big Eddy goes away?"

"I've got an idea," said Danny. "There's got to be stuff in all of those cardboard boxes downstairs that we can use . . ."

Christiana set her costume head down. "An idea for what?"

"Big Eddy was trying to scare us, right? So we're gonna turn around and scare *him.*"

He paused dramatically. "It's time for Operation Mongoose!"

"I think we're getting away from the point here," Danny said.

"Can we call it Operation Dark Thunder instead?" asked Wendell.

"No," said Danny, somewhat annoyed, because Operation Dark Thunder was a way cooler name.

"You know, Operation Dark Thunder is a way cooler name," said Christiana.

"We're calling it Operation Mongoose! Now shut up and grab some stuff to scare bullies with!"

A CALL FOR MOMMY

Wendell was nervous. It had been a bad evening, and they were about to play a joke on Big Eddy that might work, but might just make him really mad.

When Big Eddy was mad, someone usually got stuffed head-first in a toilet.

Danny crept back across the room, and listened at the window. Apparently Big Eddy was still out there, because Danny quickly turned back and waved a hand at Wendell. The iguana waved to Christiana.

Operation Mongoose was under way.

Christiana stomped a foot down on the squeaky board, which let out a scream like a dying cow.

CREEEEEEEEAAK!

"What was *that*?" Jason yelped. His voice seemed to suddenly come from farther away, as if he'd jumped back. Danny grinned and waved to Wendell.

Wendell stood in the middle of the room, holding a device cobbled together from an old jump rope and a rusty tin can they'd found in the cellar. He grabbed the rope and began whipping the can around over his head in a circle.

An eerie keening began as the can picked up speed, rising in pitch as Wendell got into the rhythm.

Danny could hardly keep from crowing with delight. The iguana said he'd read about it in a magazine—it was called a "bull-roarer" or something like that—and he thought he'd be able to make one, but he hadn't been sure it would work. You were supposed to use wooden planks, not tin cans and old jump ropes.

Nevertheless, it was working beautifully.

"That's not normal!" Jason yelled. "It's a ghost!"

"Shut up!" yelled Big Eddy—whether at Jason or at the noises coming from the house, it was hard to tell.

Christiana joined in with another series of shrieks from the floorboards.

"I want to get out of here!" said Jason. He was definitely farther away now. It sounded like he'd run clear off the porch.

Danny decided it was time for him to contribute. Holding the big copper bowl in both hands, he slammed it hard against the wall.

Danny pressed his ear to the crack in the boards again. The sounds of footsteps, and of Big Eddy yelling "Shut up, shut up, *shut up!*" were fading into the distance. He felt the warm glow of a job well done.

WE DID IT!

WOOHOO!

UH, GUYS ...
LITTLE HELP?

It actually took longer to extricate Wendell from the bull-roarer than it had to scare the bully off, but nobody minded.

Unfortunately, whatever Big Eddy had done to jam the doorknob, it was still jammed. Danny stood on the couch and twisted the knob as hard as he could, but nothing happened.

"Well, crud."

"We should still try upstairs," said Christiana.

"What if Big Eddy's chameleon buddy is still up there?" asked Wendell.

Danny grinned. "Then he's probably scared out of his mind."

They picked up their bags of candy and Christiana's costume head. Danny didn't even begrudge the fact that the rat had gone through his bag and made off with most of the Tootsie Rolls.

The only brief scare came when Wendell bent over to get his candy and stood up into a huge cobweb.

"It's just a cobweb," said Danny wearily, pulling the strands off his friend. "It's not like it's the ghost."

"And now we know it wasn't a ghost at all," said Christiana, "it was Big Eddy."

"I'm still not entirely sure of that," said Wendell, scraping off the last of the cobwebs. "I mean, Big Eddy couldn't have done anything about that painting."

"We probably just weren't seeing it clearly because of the dark," said Christiana. "Maybe it was one of those optical illusions that look different when you look at them from different angles. Anyway, haven't you heard of Occam's Razor?"

"Can you kill ghosts with it?" asked Danny.

"Well . . . I suppose *metaphorically* . . . Well, anyway, Occam's Razor is this principle that the fewer assumptions you have to make, the more likely you are to be right."

Christiana rubbed her snout. "To assume that it's ghosts, we have to assume that ghosts exist—despite centuries of failed attempts to prove their existence—that there's one here, that it's playing tricks on us for some unknown reason . . ."

Danny and Wendell waited.

"But if it's Big Eddy, all we have to assume is that Big Eddy was here and he's a jerk."

"I believe *that's* been proven conclusively," muttered Wendell.

"So there." Christiana dusted her hands. "No ghosts needed."

Danny rolled his eyes. "What is your problem with people believing in ghosts, anyway? I mean, wouldn't the world be *cooler* with ghosts?"

"The world would be cooler if there were no bullies and it rained candy, but that doesn't mean it's gonna happen."

"Sheesh," said Danny. "Lighten up already!"

Christiana sighed. "Look, it's just . . . sloppy

thinking, okay? Like a hundred years ago, there were people called Spiritualists who claimed they could talk to ghosts, right? So they'd take money from these poor people who'd lost their kids or their husbands or whatever and claim they were talking to the ghosts of their dead kids. And the Spiritualists were all frauds, but they'd just bleed those poor people dry, and leave them with no money and their family still dead, and it was all just sad and stupid."

OKAY, YEAH, THAT'S PRETTY AWFUL, AND I HOPE THEY WENT TO JAIL . . .

It seemed to Danny that the fact that the Spirit-whatsit people had been jerks who lied about talking to ghosts didn't necessarily mean ghosts didn't exist. He'd once tried to convince his father that the tracks left in the lawn by some careless handling of a bowling ball were the work of a rogue elephant, and the fact that it hadn't been a real elephant did not mean that no elephants anywhere were real.*

Christiana did not seem entirely reasonable on the issue however, and anyway, standing around arguing about long-dead con artists was not getting them out of the house any faster.

"It'd be awfully hard. And sticky," said Wendell suddenly.

They both looked at him.

"If it rained candy," said Wendell. "It'd be worse than hail, because it wouldn't melt. You'd get all those dents in your car, and then there'd be candy stuck to everything, and you couldn't even eat it because it would have been all over the ground."

---

*His father had grounded Danny immediately—not, he said, for the bowling ball marks, but for insulting his intelligence with the elephant bit.

"And have you ever gotten hit with hail? It hurts! It's like a little chip of glass! Imagine if you got whacked with a jawbreaker or something!"

Christiana looked at her bag of candy as if she was thinking of whacking the iguana with a jaw-breaker *right now*.

"We'd get reinforced umbrellas," said Danny. "And instead of rain gutters, we'd have candy gutters."

Danny was mulling over this mental image when they reached the kitchen and Christiana let out a hiss.

Wendell kept going for a couple of seconds—something about pollution causing acid candy rain—then noticed what the other two were looking at. His voice choked off with a squeak.

The hallway was still empty and clown-free, but the wallpaper was suddenly oozing something that looked like blood.

Christiana stood there with her hands on her hips, glaring at it.

HMMPH!

Wendell didn't really know what to say. It hadn't been an attractive wallpaper to begin with, but the ooze didn't help. On the other hand, it wasn't quite as scary as it could have been. It was so over-the-top, midnight-movie-on-the-oldies-station cheesy that it seemed more like a Halloween decoration than an actual horror.

He was careful not to touch it, though. Might be a biohazard. The house couldn't possibly have had its shots.

Danny, being Danny, put out a finger and poked it.

Christiana wiggled her cilia at him.

"Eggs or blood . . . I don't really see how Big Eddy could have done that," said Wendell.

"Let's just keep moving," Christiana said, who clearly needed a minute to think of a reasonable explanation.

Bags of candy in hand, the three of them crept toward the kitchen, but things didn't look any better in there. An eerie green light oozed from one of the corners of the ceiling. It made a thin bright line, ran down the wall to the kitchen counter, then skittered over it and down onto the floor. The light traced the edge of a floorboard, zigzagging across the floor until it reached the stairs.

"What . . . is . . . *that*?" squeaked Wendell.

"Maybe it's somebody with a laser pointer?" whispered Christiana.

It didn't look like any laser pointer Danny had ever seen. The light wasn't at all jittery or flickery. Instead it oozed like glowing green honey up the stairs, flowing over each step, and vanished finally into the second floor.

"*That* wasn't normal," said Danny. "Cool, but not normal."

"I knew there were ghosts!" hissed Wendell. "I knew it, I knew it!"

"It wasn't a ghost!" snarled Christiana. "It was Big Eddy! We saw him!"

The last word wasn't quite out of her mouth before the now-familiar voice whispered, *"I'm hungry . . ."* It seemed to be coming from behind the wallpaper. Wendell let out a yelp and tried to hide behind his pillowcase.

"You think *this* is Big Eddy too?" Danny didn't bother to hide his disbelief. Hammering on walls was one thing. Big Eddy was good at hammering on things—walls, nails, smaller kids who wouldn't hand over their lunch money . . .

Setting up eggs and sophisticated light shows was something else entirely. Danny wasn't sure that Big Eddy knew how to use a light switch, never mind whatever that green light had been.

IT HAS TO BE! I'LL PROVE IT!

She stomped toward the stairs.

She was halfway across the kitchen, and Danny and Wendell were giving each other should-we-follow-her/what-are-you-crazy looks, when a sound came from down the hallway behind them.

It was a very ordinary sound. Under normal circumstances, it might even have been a funny sound.

It was the sound of a toilet flushing.

Christiana stopped as if she'd run into a brick wall.

All three of them turned.

Footsteps creaked down the hallway and halted in the entryway to the kitchen.

Something stood in the doorway.

Something glowing.

Something *grinning*.

It was the clown from the painting.

WHEN CLOWNS ATTACK

The flashlight wasn't on it, but it didn't matter. The clown shone in the dark as if it were made of fireflies.

Wendell grabbed Danny's shoulder so hard it hurt. Danny didn't blame him. His stomach felt like someone had wrapped an invisible hand around it and squeezed.

The clown looked at each of them in turn, its painted eyes settling finally on Christiana. Its mouth yawned open. It had a great many teeth, and they were very long and sharp.

YOU'RE SCARED OF CLOWNS.

Then it giggled.

It was a high, humorless giggle, and it stayed in the air a lot longer than it should have, like a crow cawing.

Christiana tried. Danny gave her credit. She really, really tried. She actually stood her ground, even through that awful giggling, even when the clown took a step forward. Danny wasn't sure if he'd be able to stand there through that, and Wendell would have been in the next county and picking up speed.

"Wanna see a trick?" said the clown, and giggled again.

Christiana didn't speak. Wendell made a noise to indicate that he very much did not want to see a trick.

The clown reached up, popped its red nose off the end of its snout, and held it in the air. "Nothing up my sleeve . . ." it said.

Then it casually popped out both of its eyeballs—Wendell yelped—and began juggling them.

It was too much for Christiana. She let out a yell of disgust and bolted around the kitchen table—*no, don't run,* Danny thought, *they can't chase you unless you run,* which made no sense yet nevertheless struck him as absolutely true—and dove behind Danny and Wendell.

The tightness in Danny's chest made it hard to breathe, but he tried to suck in air anyway. If the clown got any closer, he was going to breathe fire. He might burn the house down, and the clown might be a ghost, and ghosts probably didn't burn, but he had to do *something.*

Meanwhile, a tiny little voice in the back of his head was going *How is he doing that? If you're juggling your own eyeballs, how can you see what you're doing?*

He gulped air. His sinuses felt smoky, but he couldn't seem to get a deep breath.

The clown, still juggling, walked to the edge of the table, across from them. "No?" it said. It

popped its eyes and nose back in, none the worse
for wear.

"Bet you can't do that," said the clown. It leaned
forward.

As fire-breathing went, it wasn't worth much. There was a lot of smoke, and the flame was better suited to a birthday candle. The clown snickered.

But there *was* a clown.

That meant there was a ghost.

That meant that his vision had been real.

Danny shoved a hand into his pillowcase, found the battered edge of the stuffed animal, and yanked it out.

You used crosses on vampires and silver on werewolves . . . maybe you used stuffed animals on clowns.

The clown recoiled. "That's *mine,*" it said in a thin, childlike voice. But instead of coming toward them, it backed away, up the stairs. The firefly light coming off it cast flickering bars of shadow across the kitchen, and then it too was gone.

Slowly, painfully, Danny's stomach unclenched. He turned. Wendell was wide-eyed, but seemed okay. Maybe if you believed that there were ghosts, it came as less of a shock to find out you were right.

"You saw it too?" asked the iguana.

YEAH.

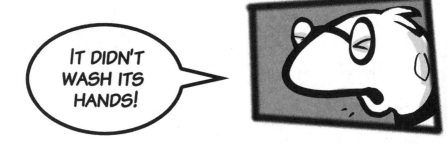
IT DIDN'T WASH ITS HANDS!

Danny couldn't think of anything much to say to that—they hadn't heard running water after the toilet flush, so Wendell was probably right. He looked at Christiana.

The crested lizard was in a bad way. She was on her knees, breathing in short, panicky gasps, and she had gripped the costume head so tightly that she'd bent some of the wiggly bits in half.

"Christiana? Christiana? It's gone!"

Danny grabbed her shoulder and shook it. "Christiana?"

She wrinkled her snout at him. "What's that *smell*?"

"Danny breathed fire," said Wendell.

It was the best possible thing that anyone could have said. Christiana's eyes focused on him with sudden intensity, and she said, "Nuh-*uh!*"

"Uh-*huh!*" said Wendell. "He totally did!"

She sat up. "Do it again," she said.

"It doesn't work like that," said Danny. "I only did it because that clown was coming at us. I can't just do it on command."

"Sure," said Christiana, in a tone that indicated she didn't believe a word of it.

"He did!" said Wendell.

DID NOT!

YOU KNOW, SINCE THERE'S A MURDEROUS GHOST CLOWN UPSTAIRS, MAYBE THIS ISN'T THE BEST TIME FOR THIS!

"I've been thinking," said Danny. "I'm not sure it's murderous."

"That clown," said Wendell firmly, "was up to no good."

"Clowns are *never* up to anything good," muttered Christiana.

Danny shrugged. "Look, I know it was scary, but it didn't hurt us. And it definitely recognized the stuffed animal."

The trio considered.

"Well . . . not all ghosts are bad," said Wendell slowly. "A lot of them—from what I've read—just want to be acknowledged, or laid to rest, or something like that. Maybe it just wants our attention."

"It's got *my* attention," said Danny. "And everything we've seen—the footsteps, the clown, the light—they've all led upstairs." He pointed upward.

The kids stood in the dusty kitchen, flashlight trained on the stairs. Nothing moved. Very distantly, through the boarded windows, they could hear the sound of crickets.

"Are you suggesting we go up there?" asked Wendell, gulping.

Danny nodded.

"Okay," said Christiana, "okay, let's say for the sake of argument—not that I believe it—that this *is* a ghost. Why would it want us upstairs?"

"But anyway, maybe its remains are up there, and we're supposed to lay them to rest."

"Do you know how to lay bones to rest?" asked Christiana skeptically.

Wendell frowned. "I've read a couple of things. I could probably wing it."

Danny slapped the iguana on the back. "My buddy the exorcist!"

"A skeleton is one thing," said Christiana. "It's bound to be less squishy than the sheep brain, anyway. But what if the . . . fine, all right, the *ghost* . . . is hostile, and it's luring us into a trap?"

Danny rubbed the back of his neck. "Well, I don't know. But I keep thinking that if it could hurt us, it probably would have already. I mean, the clown was *right there,* and none of us ended up murdered."

"Yeah, but it wasn't nice at all," said Wendell. "It might not be trying to hurt us, but it sure is trying to scare us."

ALTHOUGH ... MAYBE ALL IT CAN *DO* IS SCARE US. IT DEPENDS ON WHAT KIND OF GHOST IT IS.

"Well, what kind of ghost is it?" asked Christiana. "Hypothetically."

Wendell threw his hands in the air. "What am I, the expert? I don't know!"

"C'mon, Wendell, you read like every ghost book in the library last week. You've got to know all about ghosts." Danny folded his arms and leaned against the table. "So what is it?"

Wendell took his glasses off and cleaned them on the hem of his shirt. "Well . . . I can tell you what it's *not*."

"That's a start," said Christiana.

The iguana began ticking off ghosts on his fingers. "It's probably not a poltergeist. I think they just throw things. There's a Babylonian ghost called an enkimmu that shows up if it isn't buried, but they live underground, and there was nothing wrong in the basement. There's a ghost from Thailand that looks like a skull that flies around with all its guts flapping around behind it—"

"*Cool!*" said Danny.

"—but we're not in Thailand and anyway, the clown didn't have its guts flapping around or anything."

Christiana, sensing a long list coming, dug into her bag of candy, pulled out a roll of Smarties, and began munching.

Wendell stopped in mid-recitation and stared at her.

WHAT? YOU WANT ONE?

"No, but the ghost might," said Wendell slowly. "In a whole bunch of cultures, you give ghosts offerings of food. They have days where you leave out meals for them, or even candy. In fact, on All Hallow's Eve, back in the old days, you had to leave gifts of food for the wandering dead."

"All Hallow's Eve?" asked Danny.

"What they used to call Halloween," said Christiana, gazing thoughtfully at the candy.

"Are you saying we have to cook the ghost *dinner*?"

Wendell shrugged helplessly. "Maybe. It might be hungry. It might want to be buried. It might want to kill us all and wear our livers as little hats! I don't *know!*"

Danny exhaled. There was still a little bit of smoke on his breath, but Christiana was contemplating her candy and didn't seem to notice.

"Well," he said. "I don't know what kind of ghost it is, or what it wants, but I do know where to find it."

WHAT'S BEHIND DOOR #1?

The trip up the stairs took longer than it should have, because nobody was willing to be the last one up the stairs—where any monsters waiting below could snatch them from behind—and nobody quite wanted to be first up the stairs, where they would be the first to meet the terrifying truth, which may or may not have been wearing somebody's liver as a hat.

Eventually, with much shoving and wiggling, they went up the stairs three abreast, although Danny noticed he was always the first one setting his foot on the next step.

They made it to the landing and nothing spectacularly horrible happened. Well, the wallpaper started oozing again, but by that point, nobody was really that worried by it.

Danny had managed to wrestle the flashlight back from Wendell, but had given him the stuffed animal instead. He had a feeling that it was going to be important.

The second flight of stairs was much shorter. The hallway at the top was moonlit, with dark doorways leading onto it.

At the very end of the hallway was a closed door.

Danny opened his mouth to say something—"Well, here we go," or "Look out, ghosts!" or maybe just "I hope this works!"—when the strange green light from before slid down the wall, wrapped once around the banister, and slipped down the hallway to the closed door. A thin light of green fire outlined the doorway, and then it faded.

"I guess that's where we're supposed to go," he said.

Wendell gulped again. Christiana looked grim.

Danny set his foot on the first step and began to climb.

He was only a single step from the top, with Wendell and Christiana behind him, when the closed door opened, slowly swinging with that thin creak of hinges found in horror movies the world over.

Wendell stopped. Danny took another step, and so did Christiana, which left Wendell standing on the lower step alone. He squeaked and crowded so close against Danny's back that the dragon nearly dropped the flashlight.

There was a brief moment of jostling on the stairs, and then Danny gritted his teeth and stepped up into the hallway.

A shivering wind seemed to swirl around him, and then every door except the one at the end of the hall slammed shut, one after the other—*WHAM! WHAM! WHAM! WHAM!* Wendell let out a shriek.

With the echoes of the slamming doors ringing in his ears, it took a moment for Danny to recognize that Christiana had come up beside him. A second later, Wendell was on his other side. The iguana looked terrified, and he was holding his bag of candy up like a shield, but he was there.

The hallway was about twenty-five feet long. The door at the end was cracked open just enough to see darkness through it.

It should have taken under five seconds to walk down the hallway and push the door open the rest of the way.

Danny couldn't swear to it, but he was pretty sure it took more like five years.

The first few steps weren't so bad. They made it as far as the first set of closed doors before the noises began.

"Hungry . . . hungry . . . hungry . . ." chanted the voice.

Something was scrabbling at the bottom of the door on their left, pawing at it the way a cat paws when it wants to get out. Danny didn't look at it. He kept his eyes locked forward and kept walking.

Wendell, being Wendell, did look. "It's got red claws . . ." he moaned.

"Keep walking," said Danny. "Don't look at it."

There was a soft *snick* as the door on their right opened behind them.

Danny didn't look at it. He did glance over at Christiana, and saw her leaning forward like a lizard in a strong wind. "I don't believe in ghosts," she hissed under her breath. "I don't believe in ghosts."

This did not strike Danny as a terribly productive statement, but if it got her down the hallway, he wasn't going to argue.

The wallpaper was now oozing so furiously that they should have been ankle-deep in egg yolk, but somehow they weren't.

They were nearly at the second pair of doors when one popped open, and the clown stuck its head out.

The clown grinned. It was inches away. It could reach out and grab him right now if it wanted to.

Just behind his left shoulder, he could hear Christiana saying, "It won't get me twice. It isn't real, it isn't real . . ."

He took another step forward. For some reason, all he could think of was Wendell saying: "It didn't wash its hands!"

"Come . . . closer . . ." the clown whispered. And then it disappeared back through the door.

Danny looked at Christiana. Christiana looked at Danny. Together they reached out and pushed open the door.

THE GREAT SACRIFICE

The ghost sat on the bed inside.

It was a very small ghost. It looked younger than any of them. It was hard to tell what species it had been—some kind of lizard, but it was mostly transparent and had only the hint of scales. An unboarded window behind it shone with moonlight, which fell through the ghost and across the dusty bed without casting a shadow on the floor.

"Trick or treat!" it cried, bouncing on the bed. "Did I scare you? Did I?"

Wendell wiped a hand over his face and made a noise that was either relief or disbelief or something in between.

"Uh . . . yeah," said Danny. "Definitely." He glanced at the other two. Christiana looked murderous. He elbowed Wendell instead.

YES. ABSOLUTELY. ESPECIALLY THE CLOWN.

OH, GOOD! I WORKED ON THE CLOWN FOR AGES. IT WAS THE COSTUME I WAS GOING TO WEAR FOR HALLOWEEN.

"I *haunt* here," said the ghost, sounding somewhat snooty (almost *exactly* like Danny's seven-year-old cousin, now that he thought about it). "This is where I died."

"Um," said Danny. What did you say to something like that? Stinks to be you? "Uh . . . sorry for your loss?"

"I missed Halloween," said the ghost. "I was sick and I wanted to go out trick-or-treating, and Mom said I could go next year. But instead I got sicker and I *died* and didn't get to go at *all*."

Just like my vision! Danny thought.

The ghost sounded peeved. It occurred to Danny that while trick-or-treating would be something he'd miss if he was dead, there were a lot of other things he'd miss more. His mom, say. His dad. Hanging around with Wendell. Comic books. Bacon. You know, the really *important* stuff.

On the other hand, he'd never been dead, so maybe things changed when you were a ghost. Still, Danny was getting a feeling that he wouldn't have liked the ghost very much when it was alive. (Then again, he didn't like his cousin much either.)

"So I come back here for Halloween every year," said the ghost. "Sometimes people come in, and I get to scare them, but usually they just run away." It bounced on the bed.

BUT THIS TIME I LOCKED YOU IN, SO YOU STAYED! SO— TRICK OR TREAT!

The threesome looked at one another.

"I think this is yours," said Danny, taking the stuffed animal from Wendell. "I found it in the basement, and—"

"Stuffy!" shrieked the ghost, and pounced.

It felt like cobwebs, maybe, or a puff of cool air when it touched him. Then the ghost had the stuffed animal, which had assumed the same odd transparency, and Danny was holding empty air.

"Stuffy?" asked Wendell, of no one in particular.

The ghost hugged the mangy stuffed animal tightly. "Stuffy! I *missed* you!"

Danny exhaled. "So . . ." he said. "You've got your stuffed animal back, so I suppose you can rest now, and we can get going . . ."

The ghost looked up from Stuffy, eyes narrowing. "No. Not yet. I said trick or treat!"

There was an awkward pause. The wallpaper split open and oozed a whole barnyard worth of egg yolk down over the baseboards.

"Why eggs, anyway?" asked Wendell.

"I hate eggs," said the ghost. "*And* mashed potatoes."

"We didn't see any mashed potatoes . . ."

"You didn't go in the closet."

Danny was getting frustrated. He'd been sure that the stuffed animal was the key, and if they gave it back, the ghost would be at rest, or at least let them go. Now he wasn't sure what to do.

"'Scuse us a minute," said Wendell brightly, and pulled Danny backward into a brief huddle.

"I think I've got it. Remember what I said about food offerings?" asked the iguana. "And that voice—it kept saying it was hungry, right?"

"We need to cook it a meatloaf?" asked Danny.

"No, dummy! It wants to go trick-or-treating," said Wendell. "Well, what's the point of trick-or-treating?"

"Candy," said Danny immediately—and then bit his lip. "Oh, no! You mean it's hungry for our *candy*?"

Wendell nodded grimly.

Danny winced. Ghosts were ghosts . . . but candy was candy!

"I think . . . between the stuffed animal and the offering . . . we might be able to buy it off." Wendell shoved his glasses up his nose. "I'm not sure if that'll lay it to rest, but maybe it'll at least let us go."

Danny grimaced. Figuring out the secret of a haunted house had been cool—a little spooky, sure, but a good Halloween kind of spooky. But giving up your Halloween candy . . . that wasn't cool at all.

Christiana, who had been silent through this whole exchange, stepped forward. "I've got a couple of questions . . ." she said.

The ghost frowned at her, but she plunged ahead anyway. "So you're a ghost. What happened, exactly, after you died?"

"I was *dead*," said the ghost. "Duh."

"Right, right. But your existence postulates the existence of some form of afterlife, so what does that entail? Clearly you can manifest visually and to a limited extent physically, but is your range constrained? Do you have a sense of the passage of time? Are there other ghosts with which you can communicate?"

Wendell was nodding, so he apparently understood this display of vocabulary, but Danny had started to flounder somewhere around "postulates the existence."

He wasn't the only one.

I DON'T KNOW WHAT ANY OF THAT MEANS, BUT IT DOESN'T SOUND LIKE CANDY.

BUT—

The ghost narrowed its eyes. A door slammed somewhere in the hallway.

Danny leaned over to Christiana and hissed, "Maybe this isn't the best idea . . ."

"But if it's *really* a ghost—the loss to science—!"

Another door slammed. Somewhere, the clown giggled.

Danny decided that he really, really wouldn't have liked the ghost when it was alive. It was probably one of those snotty little kids that threw tantrums on the floor of the grocery store because their mom wouldn't buy them a gumball.

He figured the clown was probably some kind of illusion, like a puppet the ghost was controlling. Maybe the ghost couldn't hurt them . . . but maybe it could.

"If we give it the candy, maybe it'll unlock the door!" hissed Wendell.

Danny had to think about this for a minute. It wasn't like they'd tried to break the windows . . . sure, they'd probably slice their arms off on the way out, but they'd have lots of candy for the hospital . . .

Christiana sighed. Her shoulders slumped. She opened up her pillowcase and dumped about half of it out on the floor.

"Offerings of food, huh?" she said to Wendell.

IT'S TRADITIONAL.

It was a lot of candy. Christiana gazed at it with longing and no skepticism whatsoever.

"You can keep the Milk Duds," said the ghost. "I hate Milk Duds."

"Everybody hates Milk Duds," said Christiana gloomily, but she swept a half-dozen little yellow boxes back into her bag anyway. Her pillowcase seemed pitifully light. It was the sort of haul you got when you were a little tiny kid going around with your mom to ring the doorbell for you.

"So that's plenty, right?" said Danny. "That's a lot of candy." He tried to hide his bag behind his back to make it look smaller.

The ghost glared at him. "I'm *really* hungry," it said. The clown giggled again, sounding as if it was right behind the door.

Christiana punched him in the arm.

Faced with this example, Danny really couldn't refuse. Christiana had extremely pointy knuckles. He upended half his pillowcase, feeling a wrench. So much sugar, lost. So much hard-earned chocolate. There were a couple full-sized candy bars in there too, the really good ones.

"Oh well," he said, "I guess it's better than Big Eddy getting it."

Wendell looked at the resulting mound of candy. He looked at his pillowcase, then up at the expectant ghost.

"This is the only really good candy I get all year," he said sadly. "My mom buys sugar-free stuff the rest of the time. And carob. I don't care what she says, it doesn't taste like chocolate at all."

Danny and Christiana both put their hands on his shoulders.

"Good-bye, chocolate," said the iguana, drawing a candy bar slowly from the bag. "Good-bye, licorice. Good-bye, lollipops. Good-bye, thing that tastes sort of vaguely like chocolate but with that weird waxy shell—"

The ghost squinted at Wendell's pie plate. "What are you supposed to be, anyway?"

"A hydrogen . . . you know, never mind. A pie salesman."

"That's a stupid costume," said the ghost.

"Yes," said the iguana, "yes, it is." He gazed into his pillowcase. "I guess it's only *pity* candy." He poured a generous quantity onto the mound.

"Hey," said Danny as the ghost burrowed into the candy, "can you open the door and let us out of here now?"

"Huh? Oh, sure . . ." It waved a hand. There was a distant creaking noise from downstairs.

Wendell did not exactly bolt, but he was out the door and headed down the hall calling "Thanks-nicetomeetyougottagobye!" with a speed better suited to a whip snake than an iguana. Christiana wasn't far behind him.

Danny paused in the doorway and turned back to say something to the ghost—he hadn't liked it, but he felt a little bad that it had died and not gotten a chance to go trick-or-treating—

The moonlight from the unboarded window fell through the place that it had been sitting, and neither ghost nor candy was anywhere to be seen.

LITTLE WHITE LIES

"Well," said Danny as they walked down the drive-way. The world seemed very bright in the glow of the streetlights. "That was an adventure."

"I'm never going anywhere near that house again," said Wendell, sadly examining the remains of his candy.

"Wuss," muttered Christiana.

OH, LIKE *YOU* ARE?

"Heck, yeah!" Christiana turned around and walked backward, gazing at the house. "I'm gonna get my dad's video camera and come back. If that really is a ghost, it needs to be documented! We need proof of what we saw!"

"It might not be there," said Danny. "We gave it candy AND its stuffed animal. Wouldn't that lay it to rest?"

Wendell shrugged. "It depends on the ghost. In some cultures, they come back for food offerings every year. There's a big festival in Mexico every year called the Day of the Dead just to feed the wandering ghosts."

Danny frowned. "If it'll be back next year, maybe we should warn people."

"Or feed Big Eddy to it."

They all snickered.

They were halfway to the sidewalk when Wendell tripped over something and fell down with an "OOF!"

"You okay?" Danny helped him up.

Surprisingly, Wendell was grinning. "I'm great! Look what I found!"

"Big Eddy must have dropped his candy when he was running off," said Christiana. "Awesome!"

They quickly split the loot three ways. It didn't quite make up for the candy lost to the ghost, but it certainly helped.

Wendell's mood improved dramatically. "So . . . Christiana . . . if you believe that's a ghost, I guess that means you believe Danny's a dragon too?"

Danny sighed.

"Don't be ridiculous," said Christiana. "Just because ghosts might be real, it doesn't mean *everything* is real. Ghosts have nothing to do with UFOs or those weirdos who think the Mayans made spaceships . . . or fire-breathing dragons. Sorry, Danny."

Danny, who hadn't expected anything else and kind of wished Wendell would drop the subject completely, stared at the sidewalk. There weren't any other kids out trick-or-treating. He wasn't sure how long they'd been in the house, but he figured it was at least an hour.

His dad was gonna kill him. Then ground him. Then kill him again.

As if in answer to his fears, the family car pulled up to the curb with a screech of brakes. His father leaped out of the car, looking relieved, terrified, and furious in equal measure.

"Thank god you're all right! Young man, you are in *so much trouble . . .*"

Danny hung his head and waited. Ghosts were one thing, but his dad on a rampage was *scary*.

Christiana looked at him, looked at his father, made a faintly exasperated noise under her breath, and stepped in front of Danny and Wendell.

MISTER DRAGONBREATH! BOY, ARE WE GLAD TO SEE YOU!

Danny blinked.

"We were following these other kids," said Christiana, managing just the faintest trace of a sob, "and we thought you were back with their parents, but then they went inside and it turned out it wasn't you after all, and by then we were a whole bunch of streets away and we didn't know how to get back—"

Wendell gazed at her in awe.

UM ...

DON'T BE MAD AT DANNY! HE WAS THE ONE WHO FOUND THE WAY BACK. WE'D STILL BE LOST WITHOUT HIM!

Danny tried to look quietly heroic. Wendell had that expression that meant he was fighting a snicker.

"Where were you?" asked Mr. Dragonbreath plaintively. "I drove up and down for half an hour looking . . ."

"Uh—" Christiana glanced at the others.

"There were a lot of cul-de-sacs," volunteered Wendell. "We kept thinking we'd found the street, and then it would end in another cul-de-sac. We probably weren't that far away, but it feels like we've been walking for *hours*."

"Well . . ." said Danny's father. He exhaled. "I suppose . . . no harm done. If you're more careful next time, we don't need to say anything more about it."

PARTICULARLY NOT TO YOUR MOTHER, WENDELL.

"So, kids . . ." Mr. Dragonbreath put an arm across the back of the seat. "I've been hearing radio reports of an escaped mental patient, with hooks for hands—"

"Oh, come ON, Dad!" Danny rolled his eyes. "We tell that one at summer camp!"

"Oh." His father considered. "So there was this ghostly hitchhiker—"

"Daaaaad!"